# SOUL
# HARVEST

# SOUL HARVEST

Edgar J. Hyde

**CCP**

ISBN 1-902012-13-5

Printed and bound in the UK

# Contents

*Chapter 1*

# New Neighbours

Billy leaned his elbows on the window sill and looked outside. It was a glorious day; the sun was shining down on Mr McKenzie, who was painstakingly raking up all the grass strewn on his freshly cut lawn.

Next door, he could see Mr and Mrs Pringle's four year old twins jump in and out of their paddling pool, squealing with delight each time the cold water soaked them afresh. Benji, their golden retriever, occasionally opened one eye to look at the twins and make sure everything was all right, but really he was too sleepy to do any more than that. He stretched in the warm sunshine and yawned contentedly.

Glancing beyond these two houses, Billy could see his other neighbours, seated on garden chairs that had been stored and unearthed for the summer months – some reading papers, others with hats tilted forwards snoozing in the sunshine. More children played by the side of the road, hurriedly licking ice cream which was melting too quickly in the heat of the sun.

Billy sighed and looked up at the cloudless sky. What a perfect day. And yet only a few short months ago he wouldn't have thought such peace and contentment possible. It had all seemed to start with the arrival of the new family in the next street . . .

● ● ●

Billy freewheeled downhill on his way home from Alex's. The two friends had been discussing tactics for next week's "friendly" with the neighbouring village's football team and Billy simply hadn't realised the time. Now he was probably going to be late. Mum worked part time in the local supermarket, and she would go mad if Billy wasn't there to supervise his little sister till Dad came home.

Pedalling furiously now, he was distracted by the sight of a large furniture van parked at the end of the street. He stopped some way behind it so that he could check for oncoming traffic more clearly.

He suppressed a smile as he noticed "curtain twitchers" observing the furniture being unloaded from the van. This was the street adjacent to the one where he lived, and he knew only too well that new arrivals were distinct objects of curiosity.

He couldn't help but notice himself, though, that the furniture seemed to belong to a different era – very heavy and dark, unlike the bright pine furniture his own mother preferred. There was a car approaching, now, so he had to wait a little while longer before continuing on his journey.

Two children stepped down from the front of the van. The boy, probably round about Billy's own age, was closely followed by a girl who Billy presumed to be his younger sister.

It wasn't until afterwards, when Billy thought back, that he realised the strange thing about the children was the quiet way they went about their business. Not a word was exchanged as they walked up the path towards their new home, no exclamations over the size of the garden, no bounding up the stairs when the door was unlocked by their parents.

When Billy and Alice had moved to their new house, he remembered distinctly how excited they had been, neither of them able to contain themselves as they ran from room to room, shouting to one another and laughing as their voices echoed in the, as yet, uncarpeted house.

The parents, too, descended from the van and Billy thought that both were strange looking creatures. The mother was small and birdlike, with a large hooked nose and the father tall and gaunt.

Billy made himself look away, almost hearing his mother chastise him for staring, and edged his bike out from behind the van. Seeing that his way was now clear, he pedalled to the end of the street and turned left into his own.

Mum was standing in the kitchen, jacket in one hand, car keys in the other, when he ran inside.

"Just in time, young man," she said, bending to kiss Alice on top of her head. "Dad will be home at the usual time, so put the pizza in the oven about ten minutes before."

"Okay, Mum, see you later," he answered her, opening the fridge to see what he could snack on meantime.

"Oh, and Billy?"

"Mm?" he looked up.

"Read the instructions this time!" she smiled as she closed the door.

He was never going to live this down, was he? Last time they were having pizza for dinner he had switched the oven on at gas mark 8 instead of 3 and it had been well and truly cremated by the time Dad got home.

(Though he hadn't told Mum or Dad, he had been so intent on reaching the next level in the new game he had bought for his Play Station that he had merely glanced at the instructions on the box, pushed the pizza into the oven and ran back upstairs to his room).

"I want some of that," said Alice, looking up at her brother from where she sat at the kitchen table.

"But you don't like crunchy peanut butter," he said, scooping some more into his mouth.

"It's not crunchy, it's smooth," his sister argued.

"So what are all these little bits, then?" he replied, sticking out his tongue to demonstrate.

"Ooh – you're gross!" Alice made a face. "Put your tongue back in – I'm telling Mum you were deliberately making me feel sick."

She stood up, pushing a stray curl back behind her ear. "I'm going outside to see what Ricky's up to – see you later."

And, with that, she turned and went outside.

"Deliberately making me feel sick! That was a good one!" thought Billy as he screwed the lid back on the jar.

Alice was the original tomboy, and *she* was the one who was gross! Ever since she'd been big enough to crawl, she'd followed him outside into the garden, picking up all manner of bugs, holding them close to her face and examining them from every angle. Nothing was safe from her grasp. Her little chubby fingers fixed themselves round fat, hairy caterpillars, her tiny pink tongue had curiously licked shiny black beetles. Worms trying to inch away and hide beneath stones were caught up and pulled in every direction – and she said *he* was gross!

He made his way upstairs, stopping at the window on the landing to look outside. Sure enough, there was Alice, clad in denim dungarees, sitting atop the highest branch of next door's tree. Ricky, though a year older than Alice, was sitting on the next branch up, no doubt having had to be helped there by the supposedly weaker girl!

Billy entered his room, switched on his PC, and entered another world. He stayed there, quite happily, until he was interrupted by the sound of the front door bell. Running downstairs, he opened the door and saw Mrs Millfield from across the road.

"Hello, Mrs Millfield, what can I do for you?" he asked.

"You can make sure," she said angrily, "that you stay on your own side of the road next time you pass my house on your bike! I'm fed up with all you kids, thinking you own the whole street, shouting and screaming, hitting footballs back and forward and expecting us old folks just to put up with it. Well I've had enough Billy Thomson, *and* you can tell your young sister that if I catch her in my back garden again I won't be responsible for my actions." And with that, she turned and left.

Billy was so gobsmacked he just stood in the doorway and watched his neighbour's retreating back. How dare she? Why, of all the cheek! He couldn't believe the tirade he'd just heard coming from Mrs Millfield – he'd thought she was a lovely old lady. He and Alice sometimes ran errands for her, and she'd always been so grateful, giving them sweets and inviting them into her house for glasses of lemonade. But now this!

"Stay on your own side of the road!"

What right did she have to say that? Just wait till he told his dad – he'd be as shocked as Billy was.

He walked back upstairs. Maybe, he thought as he reached his room, Mrs Millfield wasn't feeling quite herself today.

*Chapter 2*

# Dad Changes Personality

By the time Dad got home, Billy had the warmed plates on the table and was just about to take the pizza from the oven.

"Hi, Dad, I'll just dish this up then go find Alice."

Before he had time to do anything, though, the back door opened and Alice burst in, sobbing loudly, tears pouring down her face.

"What's wrong Alice?"

Billy put down the pizza cutter and went to his sister. Alice hardly ever cried, and he knew that whatever had happened must have been pretty bad to upset her as badly as this.

"What is it, Sis?" he asked gently, bending towards the young girl. "Are you hurt?"

"No, I'm not hurt," she gulped between sobs. "It was Mrs Millfield, Billy, you should have heard the things she said to me, and all because I went into her garden to try and find my tennis ball."

She sniffed loudly and wiped her nose on the arm of her T-shirt.

"It was unbelievable," said Ricky, who had followed Alice into the kitchen. "She was shouting at us and waving her hands about – at first we didn't think she was talking to us – she's never done anything like this before."

Billy sat down on one of the kitchen stools, holding Alice's hand tightly.

"That's really strange, you know, because she came here earlier to tell me not to go near her side of the road, or her garden, and I was starting to think that maybe she'd had a bit of a brainstorm. This whole episode's so out of character for her."

Alice was fiddling with the strap of her dungarees.

"She said if she ever set eyes on me in her garden again she wouldn't be responsible for her actions. She said she was sick of me acting like Miss Goody Two Shoes running errands for her, that she had got to hate the sight of me, and that maybe I should remind someone that I was a girl and shouldn't wear these stupid dungarees any more!"

Her voice quavered on the last few words and Billy looked up at Ricky.

"She did, Billy, she said all those

things," he offered by way of confirmation, "and a lot more besides."

Billy looked round towards his father, but there was no-one there.

"He must have gone into the living room," he thought.

"Okay, Ricky, you can go home now, thanks for bringing Alice back safely. Come on Alice."

He tried to clasp her hand again, but she dug both hands into her pockets and attempted to look brave.

Knowing she was trying hard to keep up the tomboy act, and afraid to lose face in front of Ricky, Billy dropped his hand and instead led the way into the living room.

His father was slumped in the chair,

remote control in hand, eyes fixed on the television.

"That's unusual" thought Billy. "Must be an early boxing match on, if Dad's in here before he's eaten."

"Dad – we have to talk to you," he began. His father barely took his gaze from the screen.

"Where's dinner?" he asked.

"I haven't dished up yet," replied Billy. "Dad, listen to me, we think there's some sort of problem with Mrs Millfield. When I was coming home from school today . . ."

"Bring me my pizza," said Dad, eyes still fixed on the TV. "I've been working hard in the office all day and when I get home I expect my dinner to be served up straight away."

Billy and Alice glanced at one another. This wasn't like Dad at all – what had got into everybody today?

Alice walked over and stood directly in front of her father, all blond curls and dirty tear stained face.

"Dad," she began, "Mrs Millfield wasn't very nice to me just now, and Billy and I think maybe she's not very w—"

"Shut up, Alice," her father almost shouted, "and get out of my way, I can't see through you."

Though he didn't hurt her, he pushed her out of the way with the back of his hand before kicking off his shoes and turning up the volume on the TV.

Alice fell back against her brother,

who stood rooted to the spot, stunned by what he had just seen and heard. Alice was Dad's favourite – always had been and always would be – yet he had just spoken to her as though he despised her! Alice's eyes filled with tears.

"Dad, what's wrong?" the boy began.

"Bring me the darn pizza, Billy, how many times do I have to say it? And bring me a beer too. Now! Bring me them now – then get out of the living room and leave me alone!"

Alice, though she had tried very hard not to, started to whimper again and chew on the strap of her dungarees, a habit left over from when she was a very small child. Dad turned the sound down low on the television and leant forward into his daughter's face. His lips formed a slow smile.

"Alice," he said softly.

Then, as the child looked at him trustingly, he roared:

"Shut your mouth and stop that babyish whining! Now get out of my sight!"

He said it with such venom that Alice shrank back from her father as far as she could go.

Hurt, angry and bewildered, Billy grabbed tight hold of his sister's hand and led her quickly from the room. Crying openly now, for her father had never spoken to her in that way in her entire life, she followed Billy into the kitchen and let him seat her on one of the stools.

"Sit there, Alice. I'll give Dad his dinner and we'll have ours here. If he comes into the kitchen we'll go upstairs to my bedroom. I don't know what's got into him tonight, but I know one thing for sure, once Mum knows how he's been acting she's going to be more than a little annoyed!"

Really angered by the events which had just taken place, Billy slapped a slice of pizza onto a plate and took a cold beer from the fridge. He placed both on a tray and went to the living room, where he could hear his father laugh heartily at a documentary (though it turned out to be about people with terrible financial problems). Leaving the tray at the side of his dad's chair, Billy made to leave the room.

"Oh and Billy," said his dad.

"Yes?" Billy turned.

"I don't want to hear Madam snivelling!"

Billy slammed the door – hard – and went back into the kitchen. He was unsure if the loud laughter which followed him was his dad's amusement at him slamming the door, or merely his pleasure at someone else's financial ruin on television.

Alice had stopped crying now and was nibbling slowly at her pizza. Billy checked the clock – only another half hour until Mum got home. Boy – what a weird day! First Mrs Millfield, which had been worrying enough, but now Dad too. He'd never seen his dad behave in such a way before, and especially not towards Alice. He'd always been an incredibly patient, kind and loving father and the events which had just taken place were so strange and out of character as to be seriously worrying.

Half an hour passed, then an hour, and still no sign of Mum. Billy put the dirty dishes into the dishwasher and he and Alice went upstairs.

"You go and have your bath, Alice. I'll be in my room when you come out. Mum should be back soon, she must have had to stay later at the supermarket for some reason. I'll keep watch for her coming home." He smiled reassuringly at his sister. "Go on, and remember to brush your teeth."

He went into his own room and

looked out of the window. It had grown dark now, and he watched the street for the headlights of his Mum's car. It wasn't like her to be so late, he thought as he sat down in front of his Play Station. From the corner of his eye, he saw a movement outside on the street. Someone, or something, was crouched on the pavement beside Mr Pringle's car. Whatever it was had begun to move from one end of the car to the other and, though he couldn't be sure, he thought he could see the glint of steel.

Was someone slashing Mr Pringle's tyres? He had just put out his bedroom light in order that he could see more clearly when Mr Johnston, another neighbour, straightened up from his position at the side of the car and began to make his way up his own pathway. Again, Billy thought he saw a flash of steel as Mr Johnston put something into his pocket, but he was too far away to make it out exactly. Mr Johnston reached his house and, as he turned to close his door, Billy was shocked by the evil and familiar smile he had on his face. It was familiar because it looked just like the smile his father had worn a short while before when he had shouted so cruelly at Alice.

He jumped at the sound of his door creaking and spun around in his chair.

It was Alice, clad in her pyjamas, scrubbed clean from her bath. Billy gave himself a little shake.

Boy – was he getting spooked or what? Surely there was no such thing as an "evil smile", and imagine jumping when your young sister came into your bedroom!

And as for spying on Mr Johnston, why he was almost getting as bad as the curtain twitchers he had seen earlier today when that strange new family had moved in. Though what was Mr Johnston doing out there, grovelling about on the pavement in the dark? Maybe the poor old guy had simply dropped something on the pavement and was crawling around in the dark trying to look for it.

"That was quick, Ally," he used his sister's pet name and stood up. "Come on, I'll read you a story if you want, and I'll bet you by the time I've finished Mum will be back home and Dad will be up here apologising."

But she wasn't home by then, and nor was she when story number two came to an end either. And, though she tried valiantly to stay awake, Alice fell asleep just before the final chapter and Billy tucked the duvet under her chin before tiptoeing out of her room and closing the door.

This wasn't like Mum at all, he thought as he went back into his own bedroom. He knew Dad hadn't moved from the living room, for he could still hear the television blaring loudly, and he wondered if Dad didn't think it strange that Mum hadn't thought to telephone to say she'd be late.

He checked his watch – 10 pm. She was at least two hours late now. He lay down on top of his bed and picked up his book. He'd wait till 11 pm then he'd go and look up the telephone number of the supermarket and give them a call. He knew there were night shift workers who went in when his mother was leaving – surely someone would be able to tell him if his Mum was still there. He plumped up his pillows and began to read. Ten minutes later, he was asleep.

*Chapter 3*

# Mum Changes Personality

Billy awoke next morning with sunlight streaming through his window and his sister shaking him roughly.

"Billy, wake up, we'll be late for school!"

Billy groaned and went to turn over in bed.

"Just five more minutes," he thought to himself, unable to open his eyes.

But as the sunlight penetrated his room, so too did his memories of last night. He sat up, rubbing his eyes and looked at Alice.

"What's happened – did Mum come home – where's Dad?"

"I don't know," replied Alice. "I was too afraid to go into their room so I thought I'd come and wake you first."

Billy sat up on the edge of his bed.

He was still wearing last night's clothes.

Blast – he hadn't meant to fall asleep, he was supposed to be waiting for Mum. This whole thing was too ridiculous for words. His sister was now afraid to enter her parents' room! He'd go and sort everything out now.

He found, though, that his steps faltered a bit as he walked along the landing towards his parents' room. He couldn't help remembering the way his father had behaved last night. Alice walked slowly behind. He knocked on his parents' door. There was no reply. He knocked again, then pushed the door slightly ajar.

She was there! Mum was home, asleep in the bed beside Dad! Billy turned back fleetingly to smile at Alice, then crept into the room to kneel at the side of the bed beside his Mum. He touched her shoulder gently.

"Mum," he whispered. "Wake up, please, Alice and I need to talk to you before we go to school."

Mum groaned and turned her back on her son.

"Mum," Billy whispered again. "Wake up, please, it's really important."

Without answering, Mum pushed back the duvet and got up. Pulling on her dressing gown, she walked past both her children and went into the bathroom.

Though he couldn't be sure, Billy thought he noticed a lingering smell of stale alcohol. Alice looked after her Mum, then she stared at her brother with despair and tears in her eyes.

Billy tried to be reassuring.

"It's all right, Ally, she's just sleepy. Let's go downstairs and start breakfast, I'm sure she'll be down in a minute."

He wished he felt as confident as his words sounded. He had no idea why Mum hadn't uttered a word. She was a definite "morning" person, always singing, always bright, the bane of Billy's life most mornings.

To brush past them both without a word like that, especially after getting home so late last night, was unusual to say the least.

He handed Alice the milk from the fridge and she poured it on top of her cereal before passing it back to him.

They ate in silence, each waiting to hear the fall of their mother's feet on the stairs, or (less hopeful) her cheerful voice calling to them from upstairs. Nothing.

Eventually Billy went back upstairs, despairing, exasperated and just a little scared. He found that the bathroom was empty and, when he crept into his parents' room for the second time that morning, he could see that his mother had returned to bed!

"Will you shut the darn door and stop creeping about the house?" his father said gruffly.

"But Dad," Billy stammered. "Aren't you going in to the office today?"

For an answer, his father picked up

a stray shoe and fired it at his son. It missed narrowly, instead hitting the door as Billy pulled it shut.

Well! He didn't need telling twice! He was out of there, as soon as he had taken a very quick shower and got dressed, he was getting out, both he and Alice. The sooner they were dressed and out of there, the better.

A mere fifteen minutes later, both children left the house.

"Are we going to school, Billy?" Alice asked.

"Yeah, we're going to school. Don't worry, I'll give you money for lunch, and we can go to the shop for juice and crisps for your break."

Billy thought it was best to keep things as normal as possible, and missing school certainly wasn't going to help anything.

"I'll meet you at 4 o'clock, don't worry, you won't have to go home on your own."

As he said the last statement, Billy thought how ridiculous he sounded – "you won't have to go home on your own" – surely your home was your haven, and yet here they were fleeing from theirs this morning. He vowed that he would get to the bottom of what was happening when he got home, and he squeezed Alice's hand reassuringly before leaving her to go to his form room.

He drew up his chair next to Alex's and turned to say "hi" to his friend.

"Gee, Alex, you look almost as bad I

feel – didn't you sleep last night?"

Alex shrugged.

"Bad night, Billy. Mum and Dad had a really bad fight, and I mean *really* bad, and I just couldn't get to sleep. Thing is, they're still fighting this morning, and trying to include me! I couldn't get out quick enough."

He shook his head, remembering.

"The things they said to one another – I've never heard Mum and Dad talk like that before, really ugly mean things. And then, on the way to school this morning, I saw those new people who moved in at the other end of the street. Real weird looking.

"Anyway, I thought perhaps the kids would be coming to this school, so I offered to walk with them if they wanted some company, someone to show them the ropes, know what I mean?"

Billy nodded.

"So the mother, she looks at me as though I'm speaking a foreign language and then hisses at me to 'get lost'. That's what she said – 'get lost, kid, we don't want your sort around here.' Then the boy, Rufus I think she called him, kicked me on the shin! Kicked me! Can you believe it? And when I turned round I could see that the girl and her mother were laughing!"

He shook his head.

"And I was just trying to be helpful. I swear, Billy, there's something strange going on here – maybe someone's put something in the water – but whatever it is I don't think I like it."

Billy didn't know what to make of this. He told Alex he was having weird problems too, but just then the classroom door opened and their form teacher arrived.

"I'll speak to you at break," he said, opening his school bag and taking out his books.

Mr Stirling, their form teacher, sat down at his desk and looked at the boys and girls seated before him. Instead of the usual "Good Morning", he said nothing. Instead he put his hands behind his head and his feet on top of the desk.

Some of the boys started to laugh, thinking he was having a joke with them, but most of the pupils were a bit nonplussed. He then took a pack of cigarettes out of his inside jacket pocket and lit one up.

"Anyone who doesn't like this can leave," he announced, startling nearly everyone.

He was smoking! In the middle of class! The teachers weren't allowed to smoke anywhere in the school grounds, never mind in the middle of class!

Billy and Alex, having been witness to strange events over the past day and a half anyway, were probably the least affected by what Mr Stirling was doing. Both of them merely packed their bags, put them into their school bags and left the classroom.

Bedlam greeted them in the

corridors. Instead of being seated quietly in their individual form rooms, schoolchildren were everywhere.

Alex managed to glean enough information from some of them to learn that only four out of a possible twenty-six teachers had turned up for work this morning, that the headmaster was rolling drunk in his office, and basically the children were all being left to their own devices.

Billy pushed his way downstairs to the corridor where Alice's classroom was situated and, finding her wandering around aimlessly, still clutching her juice and crisps, took tight hold of her and the three children left the school together.

Ricky was outside in the playground too, only he was hopping mad.

"What's wrong with you, Rick?" asked Alex.

"What's wrong?" spluttered Ricky. "Look at this," and he held up a raggedy, torn schoolbag. "Mum bought me a brand new Adidas one for the start of term, and some of the other kids in the class thought it would be a great laugh if they grabbed it off me and left me with this piece of rubbish! I've got all my money in that bag. Mum will kill me. But, really, there was nothing I could do. They overpowered me."

"Who were they?" asked Alice, defiant little hands on hips.

"That's just it," replied Ricky, "the two ringleaders were like my best mates up until this morning. Part of the reason I couldn't hit back was shock, I think."

Just at that, the culprits ran past swinging the Adidas bag above their heads and laughing heartily.

"Hey, Ricky, thanks for the bag," one shouted. "We don't need this, though."

He took a drinks can from inside the bag and threw it at Ricky's head. It hit his target, the jagged edge of the ring pull catching the side of his brow.

"Ow!" he yelped, putting his hand to his head.

Blood oozed from the cut, and Billy searched his pockets frantically for a handkerchief to stem the flow. Alex ran after the boys, shouting at them to stop, but they only laughed and shouted obscenities.

"Do you want some of the same?" one of them shouted, and Alex decided he'd better keep back just in case they pulled some other kind of stunt.

He walked back and rejoined his friends.

"Are you all right, Ricky?" he asked, noting the handkerchief was covered with dark red blood.

"Yeah, I'm okay. Maybe I should go report this to the headmaster, or one of the other teachers, for that matter."

"No point, mate," said Billy wryly. "By all accounts, the Head's drunk, and the teachers that did turn up this morning couldn't care less about what happens to us."

He checked his watch – 9.30 am. Since just after 4 pm yesterday, the whole village seemed to have gone stark staring mad. He didn't really know what to do next, but he did know that the little group round about him were looking towards him for guidance. They needed a leader and, like it or not, he was going to have to lead them, though quite where they were going he had no idea!

The local park was where they went eventually, having stopped to buy more crisps and juice on the way. By the time they got there, everyone was back to their normal selves, joking and laughing, and behaving almost as though nothing untoward had taken place.

The park was busy; some of the other children had obviously had the same idea as them.

The swing park for the younger children was cordoned off from the rest of the park, but today this hadn't stopped the older children from entering. They were standing on swings that were built for children more than half their age, the seesaw had been broken as a result of at least ten children standing on it, and two boys were in the process of painting the chute with bright red paint, so that the next child to slide down would be coated in it. The noise level of children squabbling and fighting was quite unbearable.

"Don't think this was such a good idea," said Alice, looking at Billy.

He nodded his agreement.

"Let's go somewhere else – there must be somewhere we can go that's a bit quieter."

And so they ended up in the

museum, huddled in a corner beside the fossil display.

There had been no museum attendant when they arrived (not surprising, in fact almost nothing surprised them any more) and none of the other villagers had found it necessary to a visit to the museum that day (also not surprising) so they had simply walked in and found somewhere quiet where no-one would disturb them.

"Okay," said Billy, "here are the hard facts:

"1. Our mum and dad," he nodded in Alice's direction, "have gone inexplicably mad.

"2. Alex's parents have gone mad, and he gets kicked in the shin by the new neighbours.

"3. Both Mrs Millfield and Mr Johnston have been acting strange.

"4. School has turned into a complete joke where wild animals roam free and chuck drinks cans at people's heads.

"5. None of us has any idea what is going on or what we should do about it."

"I've noticed something else," put in Alice.

The boys looked in her direction.

"For what it's worth, we four seem to be the only ones behaving normally. When you think about it, everyone else has been acting really weird since yesterday afternoon, like Billy says, except for us."

The boys digested this piece of

information, agreeing with what Alice had said.

"So what do you propose we do?" asked Ricky.

"What's that saying again?" she looked at her brother. "When in Rome . . ."

"You mean behave like a lunatic as well?" Billy looked at her questioningly.

"Well, yes, I mean just until we've figured out what's going on."

She looked at the others, who remained silent. Pulling open packet of crisps, she popped one into her mouth.

"That is, of course, unless anyone has any better ideas."

*Chapter 4*

# More Trouble

Things got steadily worse.

When the children returned home, Dad was having a stand up fight in the garden with Ricky's father. Knowing he would probably only worsen the situation by trying to pacify the two adults, Billy simply walked past them and into the house, taking Alice with him. Mum sat, legs tucked beneath her, in the front room.

"Obviously not going to work today, then," thought Billy, though he knew better than to voice his thoughts.

She ignored both children as they came into the room, instead concentrating on the magazine she held in front of her. There were at least four dirty coffee cups surrounding her chair, and empty biscuit wrappers were scattered on the floor. The cigarette she held in her hand (she had stopped smoking more than ten years before) she flicked carelessly onto the carpet, a small pile of ash already starting to build up just in front of where she sat.

Alice turned and left the room, going instead to the kitchen. Billy followed closely behind.

They made a pile of cheese and tomato and peanut butter sandwiches, poured glasses of milk and, grabbing some chocolate biscuits, piled everything onto a tray and went upstairs.

On reaching the top landing, they found there was barely enough room for them to manoeuvre. Everywhere they looked was stacked with CDs, videos, boxes full of books, a motley assortment of watches thrown carelessly into a large plastic wrap, jars and jars of coffee. On and on the items stretched until the children didn't know where to look next.

"What on earth . . .?" mumbled Billy.

They managed to get into Billy's room and, through the open window, were able to hear that the fight between their father and Ricky's still waged furiously. Alice looked out from behind the curtain, and could see that her dad's nose was bleeding.

A small crowd of neighbours had gathered but, rather than attempting to stop the fight, they were shouting words of encouragement and egging the two men on.

Ricky's dad was enraged.

"Those watches were mine" he was shouting. "I saw them first – you had no right taking them from Lawsons."

"Lawsons – that's the jewellers in the High Street isn't it?" Billy looked at his sister for confirmation.

Alice nodded, not yet understanding what was going on.

"First come, first served," shouted back Billy and Alice's dad, pushing Ricky's dad so that he tripped and fell over the small fence which separated their two gardens. "If you hadn't been so intent on looting the camera shop, you might have beaten me to it, but as it is I've got lots of time on my hands and you haven't."

He laughed heartily at his joke.

Ricky's dad picked himself up from his garden and spat furiously on the ground. The crowd cheered, seeming to enjoy the fight the dirtier it got.

"It'll be a cold day in Hell before I ever speak to you again Ritchie Thomson!" he told Billy's father. "Honour among thieves, I thought they said – obviously not where you're concerned."

And with that he turned and walked inside his house, banging the door loudly before he turned the key.

Alice looked at Billy, wide eyed.

"They stole all this stuff?" she asked him. "Is that what they mean – they're actually fighting over the spoils they took from the shops?"

Billy nodded.

"That's what it looks like, Ally. Come on, come back from the window, we have to talk about this."

As Billy drew his Alice back, he noticed Rufus, his sister and parents standing at the edge of the crowd. They stood out from everyone else, mainly for two reasons:

1. They were dressed from head to foot in black, despite the warm spring sunshine and

2. They were the only members of the crowd who were not jeering. They merely stood silently, smiling.

Billy thought that the family might have looked in their direction, but he couldn't be sure. He was uneasy enough, though, to want to draw the curtains in the room before he and his sister sat down to try and eat.

Alice made a last valiant attempt at finishing her sandwich.

"It's no good, Billy," she said. "I just don't seem to have any appetite."

Billy finished drinking his milk.

"I know what you mean," he said, although he himself had managed to devour three sandwiches and two chocolate biscuits!

"What are we going to do then?" she asked, looking at her brother.

They'd been silent for the duration of their meal, if you could call it that, and Billy had been able to collect his thoughts. He cleared his throat.

"The way I see it," he began, "all this weird stuff started the day Rufus and his weirdo family moved into the village. I think that somehow they have a connection with what's been going on, and I also think that if we want any answers we have to get over there and check out their house."

Alice's eyes widened.

"You mean go inside the house?" she asked. "We can't do that – they might catch us."

Billy shook his head.

"We'll scout around outside first, see if we can find any clues. Who knows what we may come up with. Let's go next door and get Ricky, then we can walk over to Alex's house."

On the way out the two children were met in the downstairs hallway by their mother.

"And just where do you think you're

going?" she demanded. "The Church Youth Club?"

Her face contorted as she threw her head back and laughed hysterically for no apparent reason.

"Girl Guides? Scouts?" she laughed again.

"I'm not going anywhere with her, that's for sure," said Billy.

He pushed Alice out of the way.

"Real little Goody Two Shoes, always wanting to make herself useful and run errands for old, helpless people. She's pathetic."

Alice looked at her brother, aghast.

When Mum threw back her head and laughed again, Billy winked quickly at Alice, and suddenly she understood what he was up to.

"Don't listen to that twerp, Mum. He doesn't know what he's talking about. Those days are well over. I'm off up to the High Street to see if there are any decent trainers left in my size – that's if the whole shoe shop hasn't been plundered by now!"

Her mum smiled and patted her arm.

"That's my girl, I knew you wouldn't let me down. Have a nice time, and happy hunting!"

Billy winked again at his sister as Mum left them to go back to her seated position in the front room.

"Well done, Sis," he whispered. "Performance of a lifetime."

Alice smiled back, picking her way through the rubbish strewn across the kitchen floor.

A normally fastidiously tidy person, her mum seemed to have gone through a complete reversal in all aspects of her personality. Empty boxes which had once held microwaveable meals had simply been discarded and lay at random intervals on the floor. Empty bottles joined the clutter, as did the dirty washing which spilled from the washing machine.

The two children left as quickly as they could and made their way next door. They had to knock twice before there was any reply. Ricky's mother finally answered.

"What?" was all she said as she looked at the children on her doorstep.

"We wanted to see Ricky," said Billy.

Her eyes were cold.

"Ricky's grounded," she said before slamming shut the door, almost catching Alice's fingers in the door jamb as she did so.

"Grounded! Well, that's great news," said Billy sarcastically as the two children left the doorstep. "Wonder what he did to deserve that."

"Ssh," said Alice. "I hear something."

The two children stood still and, sure enough, there it was again. A faint banging noise could be heard in the garden, but where was it coming from? Alice glanced up at Ricky's window; there was no-one there.

"The garden shed, Billy, the noise is coming from the garden shed."

Luckily for them, the key had been

left in the lock and they unlocked the door quickly. Though it was pretty dark in there, they were just able to make out Ricky seated in the far corner of the shed, eyes wet with tears, still methodically banging on the wall with his shoe. Alice ran and knelt beside her friend.

"Oh, Ricky, are you okay? What happened – who locked you in here?"

Ricky looked up.

"I'm so glad you're here, Alice, I thought I'd be locked inside forever!" he shivered. "Mum and Dad locked me up, that's who. Can you believe they did this to me? And for no reason?"

He wiped his eyes.

"I know you must think I'm a baby," he said to them both, "but I've been so afraid. Apart from the darkness, when it's really quiet I can hear scuttly things running about."

Ricky shuddered when he thought about what horrible scaly creatures might be lurking in the shed, just waiting to crawl up his trouser legs or into his nose and ears. He braced himself and continued.

"I decided to bang on the wall, hoping to scare the creepy crawlies into keeping away from me, the bonus being of course that you heard me! But do you know the worst thing?"

He looked at them both with desperate eyes.

"The worst thing of all is that Mum *knows* how scared I am of creepy crawlies in every shape and form – she *knows* and yet she still let Dad lock me in here, in fact she helped him do it."

Billy put out his hand to help the boy to his feet.

"She's not herself just now, Ricky. I don't think she, nor anyone else in the village, really knows what they're doing right now. Come on, let's get out of here before they find us. We have to get to the bottom of this before anyone really gets hurt."

They left the darkened shed, locking the door behind them as they did so. Billy walked on in front and Alice stood on tiptoe to whisper in her friend's ear.

"And I don't think you're a baby at all, Ricky, I think you're one of the bravest people I know."

He smiled gratefully at her, then all three walked to Alex's house.

*Chapter 5*

# The Book

It wasn't yet completely dark, though dusk had started to fall, and this gave an eerie look to the outside of the new neighbours' house. The plaque which had been affixed to the door just above the bell read "Grimaldi."

"The Grimaldi family," said Billy. "Grim, all right, by the looks of them."

He opened the bag he had brought with him and emptied out the contents.

"Halloween masks!" exclaimed Alex. "What are we doing – trick-or-treating the Grimaldis?"

They each took a mask, looking at Billy curiously.

"No, Alex, we're not trick-or-treating. What we *are* doing is disguising ourselves. So far as I can see, we're the only people in the village not affected by whatever's going on here. By remaining anonymous, we have a much better chance of finding out what's causing everyone to turn so nasty, and possibly even a way of stopping it altogether. By putting these masks on, we could be anybody, don't you see. We could just be some wild kids out for the night, scaring people half to death by jumping out on them. Only *we* know better, don't we – we know we're the vigilantes!"

"The vigilantes," Alice breathed. She loved the sound of that – it was so romantic. The four of them out here not just to save the village, but possibly even the world!

Alex's voice brought her back to reality.

"Okay, then, Billy, what do you want us to do?"

"Snoop for now, I think," replied Billy. "Look in the grounds first to see what you can see, then try the windows. Alice and I will take the back of the house and you two guys take the front. We'll meet back at Alex's house in fifteen minutes. Okay?"

Everyone nodded.

"Masks on then, and be careful."

Billy and Alice crept stealthily to the back of the house – he wearing the head of a 70-year-old man complete with white flowing wig and beard, she sporting a clown's head resplendent with purple curly wig. Somehow the clown's smiling face seemed just a little bit spooky in the twilight.

As they turned into the back garden, something brushing against Billy's leg made him gasp. He managed not to cry out. Glancing down, two green eyes started up at him. It was a black cat, its hair standing on end, claws bared ready to attack. This was just too creepy for words, darkened houses, black cats, whatever next? He pressed his back against the wall and continued to edge to the back of the house. The cat remained motionless, its green eyes never leaving Billy for an instant.

The grounds and gardens surrounding the Grimaldis' house looked innocent enough, though Billy wasn't really sure what he should be looking for anyway – dead bodies? He wondered if maybe they were all being a bit melodramatic about the whole affair, but then he remembered his parents' behaviour and all the stolen goods that lined his hall at home, and he decided that he was not.

He could see Alice standing on tiptoe peering into one of the rooms. He looked into the other one, but all the lights were out and he could see nothing. He crept over to join Alice.

"I can't see anything," she whispered, "but I can hear voices."

Billy listened too and, just at that moment, an upstairs light was switched on, casting light on the farthest away part of the garden. The children kept deathly silent, almost afraid to breathe. The upstairs window was slightly ajar, but they couldn't make out exactly what was being said. They could hear the mother and father's voices, though, and both strained to try and catch odd words.

"Almost ready . . . turn that page . . . four more . . ."

"It's no good, Billy," Alice said quietly. "I'll have to go up there."

Billy looked at her in horror. Alice was no longer looking at him, but was staring instead at the drainpipe which led from where they stood up to the top of the house.

"Oh no, Alice," her brother hissed back. "There's no way you're going up there. I know how you love to climb, and I know how agile you are, but we're not talking trees here. We're talking drainpipes, we're talking the

Grimaldi family, and how do you think they're going to react when they see a kid wearing a clown mask peering through their window?"

Alice didn't answer immediately. She dropped her gaze from the drainpipe and turned to her brother.

"What do you suggest then, Billy? We've come this far – do you just want to leave and go back home now – back home to Mum and Dad and a house full of stolen goods?" She sighed. "Some vigilantes! Don't you see – we have the chance right now to find out what's been happening to our family, and our friends. Maybe, Billy, just maybe, we've been given the chance to make a difference, maybe we can stop this evil from spreading."

Billy thought for a moment, looking first from his sister to the drainpipe, then back to Alice again.

She was right, of course, and they both knew it, and this might be the only chance they'd be given to try and set things to rights.

"Okay, Alice, if you're sure you can do this. I'm right behind you. In spirit, that is," he smiled, though she couldn't see his smile from behind his mask. "Go on," he patted her shoulder, "but be careful."

Alice turned and positioned both hands on the pipe. Then using the skill she had called on many times before, though on far less dangerous missions, like running away from Ricky, she wrapped her feet as far round the pipe as she could and began her ascent.

Billy stood with bated breath, amazed, as always, at the agility and strength of his little sister, and crossed the fingers of his right hand tightly.

The voices were louder now, and Alice was almost level with the window. The drainpipe was slightly to the right of it, and Alice had to lean over in order to get a clear view of the inside of the room.

The Grimaldi children were not there, only the grownups. They sat side by side, adjacent to a large oak desk. On the desk was one of the biggest books Alice had ever seen. It was bound in black leather, and bore the words "Soul Harvest" then, underneath, "Glosserton", the name of their village, on the front.

When Mr Grimaldi's bony fingers opened the book, Alice could see that each page was filled with columns of handwritten words.

She couldn't help but notice that the Grimaldis were both still dressed completely in black, outer garments as well, and she wondered if they did not find the night air too warm dressed in such a way.

Mr Grimaldi was turning the pages of the book, "greedily" was how she would later describe his actions to Billy, for indeed that seemed the only appropriate word for her to use. He ran his finger excitedly down each column, pointing things out to his wife. She, too, seemed agitated, almost itching to turn the book's pages by herself if her husband did not do it quickly enough.

At first Alice couldn't understand what was being said, or rather make any sense of it. It seemed to her as though Mr Grimaldi was talking about farming, because of the words he used.

"And so you see, my dear, we have ploughed the fields, the seed has been scattered, and now it is almost time for harvest."

Alice pressed her face even closer to the window and could see that each column contained a long list of names, some of which were familiar to her.

Mrs Millfield's was there, as was Mr Johnston's, some school teachers she recognised, and then she came across her dad's. Mr Grimaldi picked up his pen – he was using one of those long feathered quills which he dipped into a bottle of ink – before adding the name of Jennifer Thomson to the book – their mother.

Mrs Grimaldi clapped her hands excitedly.

"Just those two brats of theirs to get now and we're almost there!" she said gleefully.

Alice could see there were only four spaces left to be filled in the book.

"They must be waiting for the four of *us*, then their book will be complete!" she thought fearfully.

Mrs Grimaldi stood up and Alice pulled her head back towards the drainpipe, hoping not to be noticed. The woman threw open the window wide, narrowly missing one of Alice's blonde curls, and gazed happily up at the night sky.

"Look dear," she said to her husband. "They're waiting patiently for the harvest, waiting and watching as we help them to reap more souls."

From his position on the ground, Billy could hear every word as Mrs Grimaldi's voice carried through the night. Following her gaze, he looked skyward and gasped so loud he was afraid he had been heard. There, hovering above the ground, truly as though waiting to harvest the crops, the *souls* of these good people, was the Grim Reaper.

The face Billy had only ever seen in books and movies was even more gruesome than its depiction. Billy was more terrified than he had ever felt in his life. The hood of the Reaper's black robe framed a grotesque face with black-rimmed sunken eyes and bloodless skin that was gaunt and skull-like. At first, its eyes appeared to be black and sightless, but the reaper directed its inescapable gaze towards the quaking boy and Billy saw that its demon pupils burned bright scarlet.

The eyes seemed to burn straight into Billy's soul. He shuddered – this was worse than he could ever have imagined. He looked upwards – Alice still held her position on the drainpipe and, as Mrs Grimaldi went back inside, she took the opportunity to slide back down to the comparative safety of the ground.

Billy caught her hand at the bottom.

"Run!" he whispered urgently. "Quick, Alice, we have to get out of here – now!"

Alice followed his gaze as he looked upward. From where she had been positioned on the drainpipe, she hadn't seen the Grim Reaper, but now she did, and suddenly she understood. A little scream escaped from her lips and Billy pulled her with him and away from the house. Turning back briefly to check that the Grimaldi family had not seen him, he saw that the sky was full of Grim Reapers, watching and waiting. He was never quite sure whether or not he imagined that the skulls were smiling.

*Chapter 6*

# The Procession and the Reapers

The two children threw themselves into Alex's porch, gasping for breath, and collapsed into a heap. Alex and Ricky were already there. Billy and Alice tore their masks off.

"You okay?" Alex asked.

Billy nodded.

"Just about," he replied. "Did you see anything out there?"

Now that he could see his friend more clearly in the light from the porch, Billy saw that he was shaking. Ricky didn't look too good either.

"Let's just say I think we probably saw what you did – in the sky? Man, were we scared!"

Alex shook his head.

"I'm not going back out there tonight, that's for sure. In fact, you're all welcome to stay here tonight, that's if you don't object to sleeping on the floor."

"A hard floor is much more appealing than what's out there," said Ricky. "I'll definitely take you up on your offer."

Billy spoke.

"I think it's probably best if we all stay together for tonight – it's just not safe out there."

"Did we find anything else out, though? Do we know what it all means?" asked Alex.

Alice, shivering partly from cold and partly from fear, related what she had seen in the upstairs room of the Grimaldi house.

"So you see," she finished, "this

book seems to contain the names of all the people who have been affected by the spread of evil – who have turned nasty, if you like – and whose souls are ready for the Grim Reapers to take. Only thing is, it looks as though they can't make a move until they have all the villagers' names in the book, and that means they need the four of us."

Ricky involuntarily checked that the door of the porch was locked.

"So what can we do?" asked Alex.

Billy sighed.

"Keep out of the way for one thing," he said. "And we also have to think how we can stop this tragedy from destroying our village. From what I know on the subject, the Grim Reaper only appears when someone is about to die, and your soul can only be taken (or *harvested*, as they refer to it), when you're dead. So, is that what they're planning to do – wipe out the whole village?"

This rather sobering thought plunged them all into silence, and they sat quietly for a while, each with their own separate thoughts.

A loud crash from outside soon broke into their reverie, and they opened the door as wide as they dared to see what was happening.

"Wow!" exclaimed Billy. "It's like a scene from the Pied Piper of Hamlin."

The two Grimaldi children were marching up the centre of the street followed by what appeared to be the entire village. The two children kept their eyes focused on the front, while the following villagers staggered under the weight of the goods they carried.

The noise from the crowd was incredible, some shouting, some yelling obscenities at people who had previously been friends, some fighting over contents of boxes. Occasionally, some of them would break free from the crowd and calmly throw a large boulder through a house window, or door. Sometimes they would climb through the broken glass and steal anything they could get their hands on, if they felt like it.

"Oh no!" said Alex, covering his eyes. "My parents are there."

"That's not all," said Billy, pointing towards the man walking just behind the Grimaldi children in the procession. "The minister!"

Though they had thought they were beyond shock, the children were stunned. If these people had the minister in their grasp, what chance did they have of staying clear?

Alex closed the door on the bizarre carnival and turned the key.

"Well," he said, "let's look on the bright side. If my parents are in the procession, it looks like we're going to have some empty beds tonight – forget the hard floor!"

Now that it was safe to do so, the children went into the main part of the house and secured all the windows and doors. They brought sleeping bags downstairs into the front room and decided it was better if they all stayed together in the same room – safety in numbers, Ricky had laughed. They sat around talking for a while, though Billy didn't seem to have much to say.

"What's wrong, Billy?" asked Alice. "You seem very quiet."

"I'm all right," he replied. "I'm just trying to think what we can do."

"And?" asked Alex.

"And," started Billy, "all I can come up with is somehow getting rid of the book. You know, the book Alice saw. It seems to be playing a central part in this; once it's full the Reapers can move in, and our names can't be added to it until we've been 'infected' by the evil around us.

"I just think that if we can get rid of

the Grimaldi's precious book then the Reapers will give up and go elsewhere, somewhere people are ready to give up their souls a bit more willingly than we are."

"But how on earth do we accomplish that?" asked Alex. "How can we even get inside that house, never mind steal the book?"

"I didn't say *steal* it" said Billy. "I said get rid of it, burn it perhaps."

"I'll do it," said Alice quietly.

The three boys turned to look at her.

"What did you just say?" asked Billy.

"I said I'll do it" she repeated.

"Oh no you won't!" her brother protested. "This is definitely far too dangerous for you. I felt bad enough last time allowing you to climb up that drainpipe and peer in windows, but to actually get *inside* the house – you have to be kidding! No – one of us will do it."

"Billy," said Alice, her voice stronger this time, "just how do you propose getting in there without the Grimaldis seeing you? Because I'm telling you it's impossible, and we all know that. There's only one way into that house, and that's in the window I was looking through. You can stand outside and wait for me if it makes you feel any better, but I'm telling you I'm going in."

She raised her hand to halt her brother's protests.

"Billy – I saw Dad's name in that book, remember, and then I watched them add Mum's. That means they're ready to take their souls, and I can't just let that happen. Anything I can do to prevent that happening, I will, and don't you try and stop me."

Alice finished speaking and bit down hard on her lip to stop herself from crying.

"She's right, you know," said Ricky. "She has every right to be concerned and to want to help."

"I know, I never said she shouldn't help. I'm just concerned for her, concerned about the dangers out there."

Alice looked her brother in the eye, with all signs of emotion gone, instead a steely determination showing on her face. Billy had seen that look before, and he knew Alice had made up her mind. When she was like this, nothing would sway her.

"Okay, Alice," he raised his hands in defeat, "you win. But you'll have to be really quick, you know, in and out, we don't have a lot of time."

For, although the children had seen the Grim Reapers and the Grimaldis follow the winding procession, they did not know how long it would be before they returned.

"We have to go now," continued Billy, "before it's too late. Alex – can you find a box of matches that we can use?"

A short ten minutes later, the children were ready to leave the house. They donned their masks once more and ran hurriedly across the road and on to where the Grimaldi's house was situated.

Though he was almost afraid to, Billy glanced up at the sky and saw that, thankfully, it was clear. They stood together in the garden.

"Now remember, Alice, straight up the drainpipe, straight in the window and burn as many pages as you can as quickly as you can, then get out. It's just a pity the book looks so heavy or you might have been able to push it out of the window and we could have burnt it outside."

Alice pushed the box of matches into the pocket of her dungarees.

"This way's easiest for me, Billy," she assured her brother. "I know I'd never be able to lift the book on my own."

She turned and started to climb the drainpipe once again, though this time a bit more fearfully than the last since she now knew what she was facing. The climb was fairly easy for her, though the window was stiff enough to give her some problems. She pushed and pulled and grunted and tugged, and the boys on the ground held their breaths and prayed. At last, it opened, and they saw Alice disappear inside the room. As she did so, the boys heard a shout come from the main street running along the front of the house. They looked at one another.

"What was that?" whispered Alex urgently.

Just then, another cry went up.

"Ricky, where are you darling?"

Ricky froze. It was his mother's voice. But she had been part of the procession. So that was where they had been going – to get Ricky from the garden shed where his parents had imprisoned him. But did this mean that the procession was returning?

Keeping close to the wall, the three boys edged around the side of the house to try and get a clearer view of what was happening.

"Ricky" she called again. "Come on dear, show yourself. I'm sorry I locked you in the shed, I won't do it again, I promise. Come out, please, and I'll show you just how sorry I am."

Ricky started to move forward. Billy quickly put a hand on his arm.

"No, Ricky, she's lying, can't you see? That's not really your mum talking – these guys would do anything to get to us. You have to stay here, else you'll give us all away."

"But . . ." Ricky started to protest, but stopped when he heard a different voice call out. This time it was his father.

"Ricky!" he shouted. "Come out now – you're worrying your mother. Come on son, we love you, please let us know where you are."

The procession wound its way up the street, some people now carrying torches which cast an eerie glow all around. The four Grimaldis, leading, seemed to be all seeing, their eyes darting in every direction, trying to find the missing children. Some of the villagers made a low humming noise, and gradually more and more people joined in. The minister who still walked just behind the front of the procession, was chanting something Billy could not quite make out. He listened more closely to the words.

"Heaven in art which father our."

He was reciting the Lord's Prayer backwards! Billy was sure he'd seen someone do that in a movie once before – he thought it had a connection with the occult, or even Satan!

He swallowed hard. The Grim Reapers, bright eyes reaching out to find the souls they wanted so badly, hovered above the procession all the time, terrifying the boys even more.

The hum of the procession now turned into words, names, and the children could not help but listen.

"Billy, Alice, come to us. Come to us now."

Billy heard his own parents' voices mingled with those of the others and, totally against his will, felt himself compelled to go towards them. Still holding onto Ricky, he grasped Alex's hand on his other side.

"No," he told himself, "I've got to be strong. If I go, we're lost. I have to wait for Alice. I have to get her out of here safely."

The procession drew to a halt just in front of the house and the chants grew louder. Alex's parents had joined the others at the front and their voices joined in the pleading. Some people were searching the surrounding area, all the while calling out the children's names.

"Ricky, come to us, child, come."

Billy thought he felt Alex push his shoulder as though towards the crowd, and he tried hard to resist.

"No, Alex," he said, "we have to stay here, please, we have to be strong."

He turned to look at his friend, but it wasn't Alex's face that stared back at him. The white skull-like face of the Grim Reaper was so close to his he could have reached out and touched it. Its eyes pierced straight through to his heart.

His two friends had left him and were walking towards their parents.

"No!" shouted Billy. "No – come back!."

The Reaper pushed him forward with his sickle, so hard that Billy fell onto the grass. He could see other Grim Reapers start to descend from the sky and surround his two friends. He struggled to stand up, for he knew that he had to run, but to where?

"Where is she?" the Reaper asked him, stepping closer.

"Who?" Billy stammered, though his voice was barely recognisable, he was so afraid.

"Alice, of course," he rasped. "It doesn't matter whether you tell us or not we *will* find her, eventually."

The Reaper put his bony, skeletal hand on Billy's arm and he shuddered.

"Come, join your friends, you don't want to miss the harvest, do you?"

Billy felt himself take unwilling steps in the direction of the crowd. He could see Alex and Ricky, each with Reapers by their sides, as though standing guard. As Billy reached the stationary procession, the chant began to change.

"Alice, come to us, my dear. Alice, we're waiting."

Billy felt utterly helpless. He could do nothing to help. He closed his eyes tightly and started to pray.

"Please, Alice, don't hear them, don't listen. They mean you harm. Stay hidden, I'll come help you. I don't know how, but I will."

He opened his eyes just in time to

see Mrs Grimaldi fall to the ground, her husband quickly getting down beside her.

"What's wrong?" he asked. His wife clutched at her throat, as though struggling to breathe. "The book – someone has the book – you must stop them."

Rising, her husband made to leave the procession and cross to the house. As he did so, the whole house burst into flames.

*Chapter 7*

# The Aftermath

The heat from the fire caused the windows to blow out, glass shattering all around. Some people in the procession were hurt. Shards of glass flew indiscriminately.

Billy, shielding his eyes from the flames, tried to fight his way back to the house. He had to reach Alice. He'd never forgive himself if she was hurt.

He tried to push his way through the crowds of people, and just then another explosion tore through the house. There were screams as more glass and pieces of flying rubble hit the now disrupted procession. Very young children were crying, some adults were lying on the ground, hurt and in pain, whilst others tried to offer them some comfort. People whose houses were nearby rushed in and out bringing with them blankets, bandages and any other items they could lay their hands on quickly.

"Billy!" called his mum, "come back – don't go near the house."

She was trying to help an old man who lay on the ground. His left leg had been hit by glass and he was losing lots of blood. Mum had tied a tourniquet and was desperately trying to stem the flow.

Billy turned back to his mum.

"You don't understand" he shouted. "Alice is in there – it was her who started the fire!"

His mum's face changed. She left the side of the injured man and ran with her son towards the house. It was completely ablaze now, there was no way anyone would be able to enter it. She started to cry, large salty tears which dripped down her face and onto her chin. She felt an arm go around her. Billy's dad had joined them, but no-one spoke. There were no words.

The Grimaldi family had completely disappeared, leaving behind them scenes of shock and devastation. Gone, too, were the Grim Reapers.

"So she was successful in destroying the book," said Billy aloud. "Though maybe just a bit too successful."

Alex and Ricky appeared by the Thomson family's side. Alex, though cut pretty deeply where he had been hit by a sharp piece of stone, was in the main all right. Ricky, too, had survived intact. He looked at Billy's tear stained face.

"Alice?" he asked.

Billy shook his head.

Just then, someone shouted his name. He turned back towards the procession, and saw a little figure clad in dirty denim dungarees, with a head of unruly blond curls, run towards him.

"Alice – you made it!" he shouted, running to her, arms outstretched. "You're all right, I can't believe it. I thought you'd been . . ."

"I did what you said, Billy," she said, crying and laughing at the same time. "Remember – in and out as quickly as you can, burn the pages and come back down the drainpipe – those were your words, and I did it, Billy, I did it."

He hugged her, lifting her clean off the ground in his delight.

"You sure did, kiddo. Well done – look – not a Grim Reaper in sight. They don't have anything to harvest any more, thanks to you!"

Mum and Dad had joined them now, and the little group all stood together, kissing and hugging. Dad ran his hand through his hair.

"Wish I could say I understood what's been happening here," he said ruefully, "but the last few days seem to be a complete blur! Very strange, very strange indeed."

Mum smiled – "I know just what you mean," she said.

Walking home a while later, when they had done what they could for the people who were injured, Billy saw the Grimaldi nameplate lying in the road. Picking it up, he tossed it into a pile of rubble that had caught fire. They stood and watched it burn, slowly.

"Hope I never hear that name again," said Billy.

Dad put his arm round each of his children's shoulders.

"Come on you guys, let's go get a pizza!"